W9-BHT-144

HOME FOR A BUNNY

By Margaret Wise Brown

Illustrated by Garth Williams

🌷 A GOLDEN BOOK • NEW YORK

Copyright © 1956, 1961, copyright renewed 1984, 1989 by Penguin Random House LLC.
All rights reserved. Published in the United States by Golden Books, an imprint of Random House Children's Books,
a division of Penguin Random House LLC, 1745 Broadway, New York, NY 10019, and in Canada by
Penguin Random House Canada Limited, Toronto. Originally published in the United States by
Simon and Schuster, Inc., and Artists and Writers Guild, Inc., in 1956. Golden Books, A Golden Book,
the G colophon, and the distinctive gold spine are registered trademarks of Penguin Random House LLC.
randomhousekids.com
Educators and librarians, for a variety of teaching tools, visit us at
RHTeachersLibrarians.com
Special Markets ISBN 978-0-375-97596-7 Not for Resale
Library of Congress Control Number: 2011925342
MANUFACTURED IN CHINA
10 9 8 7 6 5 4 3 2 1

This Imagination Library edition is published by Golden Books, a division of Penguin Random
House LLC, exclusively for Dolly Parton's Imagination Library, a not-for-profit program designed
to inspire a love of reading and learning, sponsored in part by The Dollywood Foundation.
Penguin Random House's trade editions of this work are available wherever books are sold.

"Spring, Spring, Spring!"
sang the frog.
"Spring!"
said the groundhog.

"Spring, Spring, Spring!"
sang the robin.
It was Spring.
The leaves burst out.
The flowers burst out.
And robins burst out of their eggs.
It was Spring.

In the Spring a bunny
came down the road.
He was going to find
a home of his own.
A home for a bunny,
A home of his own,
Under a rock,
Under a stone,
Under a log,
Or under the ground.
Where would a bunny find a home?

"Where is your home?"
he asked the robin.

"Here, here, here,"
sang the robin.
"Here in this nest is my home."

"Here, here, here,"
sang the little robins
who were about to fall out of the nest.
"Here is our home."

"Not for me," said the bunny.
"I would fall out of a nest.
I would fall on the ground."

So he went on
looking for a home.
"Where is your home?"
he asked the frog.

"Wog, wog, wog,"
sang the frog.
"Wog, wog, wog,
Under the water,
Down in the bog."
"Not for me,"
said the bunny.
"Under the water,
I would drown in a bog."

So he went on
looking for a home.
"Where do you live?"
he asked the groundhog.
"In a log," said the groundhog.
"Can I come in?" said the bunny.
"No, you can't come in my log,"
said the groundhog.

So the bunny went down the road.
Down the road
and down the road he went.
He was going to find
a home of his own.
A home for a bunny,
A home of his own,
Under a rock
Or a log
Or a stone.
Where would a bunny find a home?

Down the road
and down the road
and down the road
he went, until—

He met a bunny.
"Where is your home?"
he asked the bunny.

"Here," said the bunny.
"Here is my home.
Under this rock,
Under this stone,
Down under the ground,
Here is my home."

"Can I come in?"
said the bunny.
   "Yes," said the bunny.
And so he did.

And that was his home.